Find out more about upcoming books online on;

https://linktr.ee/Carrie_Weston

Other books by Carrie Weston

The Xander Chase Series

(YA CRIME FICTION/FANTASY MASH)

1. Xander Chase and the Unicorn Code

– 2. Xander Chase and the Lost Wing

-3. Xander Chase and the Battle for Deaths Throne

A Dark Fairy Tale

(Fantasy fiction)

- P.E.T empathiser's PREQUEL BOOK 0.5

-Pet Empathiser Team BOOK 1

-FRACTURED BOOK 2

-The Fabric of Magic Book 3

More - Coming soon!

A Dark Fairy Tale

P.E.T empathiser's

Copyright © Carrie Weston 2021

This novel is a work of fiction. Names, characters, businesses, places, events and incidents are either the products of the author's imagination or used in a fictitious manner. Any resemblance to actual persons, living or dead, or actual events is purely coincidental.

All rights reserved in all media. No part of this publication may be reproduced, stored in retrieval system, copied in any form or by any means, electronic, mechanical, photocopying, recording or otherwise transmitted without written permission from the author and/or publisher. You must not circulate this book in any format. Any person who does any unauthorised act in relation to this publication may be liable to criminal prosecution and civil claims for damages.

For permission requests, please contact:
authorcarrieweston@gmail.com

Produced in the United Kingdom.

C.Hollywell Illustrations shall receive credit in any distributed version of the work as the illustrator, in such places as are customary and usual within the trade for the type of work. C.Hollywell warrants that the materials delivered herein are the original work of C.Hollywell and that the same do not violate any copyright, trademark or other protection of intellectual property by C.Hollywell

All rights reserved in all media. No part of this publication may be reproduced, stored in retrieval system, copied in any form or by any means, electronic, mechanical, photocopying, recording or otherwise transmitted without written permission from the Illustrator. You must not circulate this book in any format. Any person who does any unauthorised act in relation to this publication may be liable to criminal prosecution and civil claims for damages.

For permission requests, please contact:
carolinehillustrator@gmail.com

Produced in the United Kingdom.

About the Author;

A bit about me, (OMG — skip this bit quickly). Okay, if you're still checking this out than you want to know something new, so here goes; I love and I *mean* love crystals. I have a huge collection and believe in their properties to aid one's self. As you probably know, I am a divorcee in her early 30's with a young son (who rocks – he did not make me write this) and a crazy springer spaniel who's grumpier than me without coffee (and that's hard). Since I was a kid (and no I don't mean a goat), I've dreamt of becoming a fully-fledged authoress.

Thanks for staying tuned

Hearts & Kisses

About the Cover Illustrator;

Caroline Hollywell Illustrator

IF YOU'RE LOOKING FOR; MYTHICAL, MAGICAL, WACKY AND WEIRD BOOK COVER ART AND ILLUSTRATIONS THEN CHECK OUT MY GALLERY; Carolinehillustrator (godaddysites.com)

I've previously had work exhibited at local Galleries, been commissioned to do cards and Art work. More recently I've illustrated the front cover of YA novel;

Xander Chase and The Unicorn Code.

Follow me on;

Facebook – Caroline Hollywell | Facebook

Instagram – Caroline Hollywell

LinkedIn – Caroline Hollywell - Y.A and Children's book Illustrator. - Freelance Illustrator. | LinkedIn

Dedication / Acknowledgements:

For my fans who are patiently waiting for the continuation of the Xander Chase series.

A special mention to Caroline who convinced me you all wanted more fairy tales-

To Weston Jr who helped create the map and also to editor Tiffany Purdon and my Alpha/beta reader.

And to Alex, for your support in creating these wonderful emails

Hearts and Kisses

Carrie

Jhonathan – Not all rules are put in place to bind us,

some are to protect us from others bindings.

1.Fairy's

"Never have I ever seen a creature stupid enough to eat the fruit of the Puinnsean tree," Shayleigh chuckled.

"Never have I seen a creature like that." Akantha retorted, eyeing the gangly pale fleshed thing with a greasy mop of coal dark hair. It stood on its tip toes to reach the fruit of the dangerous wild forest.

"A fawn." Shayleigh deduced, "that's what it is. See how it wears only rags." She smiled proudly around sharpened fangs.

"Do they not have hooves for feet?" Inquired Akantha.

"Hmm. I suppose they do." She conceded. "What then would you call it?"

"Well, it's been a long time since I've heard stories of such a creature, but maybe; if the stories are true, it is a human-being."

"A Bean." She placed a hand to her chin and stroked her curling horn. "Like that which grows from the vines in the summer court?" she mused. Unsure, Akantha leapt to a tree branch closer to the creature, tilting her head until her pale silver hair hung like a curtain at her shoulder. Soundlessly Shayleigh advanced beside her, her talons gripping the thick coil of the branch.

"Or perhaps it is that toy the Queens pets chase- the one that jumps whilst it runs and rolls."

"Perhaps," Akantha agreed. "But then the Queen would have her guards searching for it would she not? For she is the only owner of such creatures."

"True. There is no sight of the royal guard within the wild forest. The trees would have whispered of their presence." Shayleigh confirmed. "What should we do?" she asked turning to the beautiful fairy perching next to her, even the board shorts and tank top- the Queen insisted all 'staff' wore- was unable to dim her allure. Shayleigh watched as her friend's long spiky wings slashed so quickly, they barely created a hum in the disturbance of air.

"We do? Well, we shall do nothing, let it be, let it eat the Puinnsean fruit. It has chosen its own demise and will be dead before the hour is past."

"Akantha, I do not think the Queen would thank us for her pets passing and we both know the trees will not stay silent." Shayleigh said cleaning her talons with a lick of her long tongue as she considered her next move.

"Agreed." Akantha hissed, all be it reluctantly.

2. Jhonathan

Jhonathan knew the fairy's were perched watching his every movement as he gorged on the magical fruit of the Puinnsean tree. He had been in the Fae lands long enough to know that consumption of the berries would bind him to the realm forever. But with nothing else to eat over the three days he had spent running from the palace guards, Jhonathan was starving. He had made it deep into the wild forest with no signs of pursuit and with the help of the P.E.T empathisers he had gotten this far. Without the group of creatures taking a political stand against the Queen, he would never have escaped. For they were the ones who swore the trees to silence about their involvement of harbouring him, leaving him free to live out his life in their woody depths. But Jhonathan wanted more, he was desperate to see his family however uncool they were. He longed to hug his mother and ruffle the hair of his little brother until he swiped at him playfully. He wanted to laugh. Something the Queen made sure he never did, by way of the bit leashed in his mouth.

He had spent months led around by a finely crafted chain that sparkled in the sunlight, creating rainbow dots that danced upon the castle's marble floor. He loved to watch the colours play, their beauty reminding him of a girl he once caught smiling at him from the recess of a corridor at school.

Jhonathan sighed in content as sticky sweet juices flooded his parched mouth, trailing tracks across his chin in his desperation to devour them. His stomach groaned around its fill and swelled amongst the frame of his body's protruding bones.

He smiled to himself, swiping at his mouth with the back of his hand. The fruit he had digested was delicious; the best he had ever tasted. But it was also deadly. He knew this for it had been the only fruit the empathisers had warned him against eating. But he was starving. He could not walk another step without sustenance. That's when he had heard the branches to the right of him groaning, a warning that he was not alone. And suddenly a plan formed in his mind.

It wasn't long until the human sagged down against the strength of the tree that spearheaded his location like a grave marker. And how apt that was, he thought, as his stomach cramped and sweat pooled in fatty droplets from his skin. The fruits magic was kicking in, poisoning his system it was the trees' defence against foraging idiots. But Jhonathan wasn't an idiot and soon, oh God soon- he begged, the fairy's would come. They were too curious not to and not one of them could pass up the opportunity of the Queens favour if they returned her beloved pet. "Soon," he muttered. *Or it would all have been for nothing. No,* he thought to himself. *That's not true. Freedom comes in many ways* and with that laying peace in his mind his eyelids dropped closed, his body slunk to one side and a slight breath wheezed from his barely rising chest.

3.Fairy's

Shayleigh and Akantha had watched the human. Contemplating the actions needed to be taken to secure their safety against the Queen's legendary rage, encase she found out they had spotted her beloved pet all alone in the depths of the wild forest, eating itself to death. Finally, they had agreed upon their next move when they tuned to see the creature barely breathing at the base of the Puinnsean tree.

"Oh, for Seelie's sake!" Akantha roared. "Look at it, it is half dead already."

"Maybe it rests." Shayleigh interjected.

"Rests? With poison filling its belly? Greedy little creature."

"Stupid creature." Her friend agreed, jumping to the dirt beneath their onlooking tree, her arm skin guiding her silently down. Akantha landed next to her with barley a buzz of her enormous wings. Shayleigh looked at them enviously, those things were deadly and yet so strong as they bent and flexed at angles unimaginable to most of the fairy's. Akantha was a Faemontis. Born in the mountains of the winter court where her shadow shading helped her camouflage against some of the deadlier fairy's. The two of them had been friends since her journey to the Seelie Queens palace where she hoped to gain a place in the royal court. But as hard as she tried, she had never fitted in with the more ethereal fairy's. Shayleigh had been in the kitchens, working as the palace's maid when Akantha came seeking the luxury of ale from the human realm to drown her sorrows. Being her usual chatty and friendly self had managed to smuggle a vase of the drink and together the two hid in the shadows, talking and spilling the secrets of their lives.

    Shayleigh blinked, picking up a stick from the forests feet and stalked towards the human. It made no sound except the gurgling rasp of breath as its lungs struggled to inflate. She poked at it, the stick wobbling its swollen abdomen. Dark eyes glared at her and she jumped back, arm skin puffed ready to fly away if the creature so much as moved. But it didn't. It just continued its pitiful breathing, and she found herself cocking her head to one side as she approached a second time.

"Shayleigh," Akantha hissed "be careful, don't touch it. The poison could transfer to you, you know your skins susceptible to the Puinnsean trees magic."

"But it's so peaceful, it-"

"Is in need of your help, not you're boisterous administrations." Akantha said, grabbing her friend's wrist before she could stroke the hair from the human's face. The fairy was too kind for their realm, she wouldn't have lasted long if fairy folk didn't think she was a relative of the Queen. A fact that Akantha had found more disconcerting than appealing at the time.

Glaring at the human complicating their days hunt Akantha sent Shayleigh to fetch kindling for a fire. The sun was already going down and the wild forest had a reputation for all things deadly creeping about at night. A fact she knew to be true when she spotted the gleaming eyes of a predator lazily watching them place small branches in the shape of a pentagram with the Queen's pet at its centre.

"This should keep us safe tonight." Akantha hissed, as Shayleigh placed the last of the kindling and began to dance and weave around the artistry. A burning blaze alighting behind the trail of her tail, its glow a yellow-green as the flames lit a shielding wall from the danger of the wild forest, without even licking at a single log. Akantha watched on in awe. It was times like this that her heritage was displayed for only royals could create fire that never ate.

    Finishing up her dance, and sealing it with a knot of tight arabesques, Shayleigh crumpled into an exhausted heap, careful to keep her distance from the poison sweating human; whose skin now sank heavily like grey stone to his brittle frame. She longed to touch him and reassure him he would live but Akantha had forbid her for fear she might contract the poisoning.

4.Jhonathan

Jhonathan's heart steadied. The poison in his veins came hurling up into his throat in an otherworldly pull that ripped it from his mouth in a splay of violet light, tinged with the bruised fruit and juices he had devoured. He sighed. He was alive. The fairy's had saved him just as he had hoped and now, he was free of the berries' death curse as well as the spell cast over the fruit of the palace. He was no longer bound to the fae realm. His consumption of its foods had been dispelled by the incantation the grey fairy cast as she danced inside a circle of earth forged from the repeated beat of her taloned feet. Her wings dipping and stretching as her long silvery hair flowed behind her like a river.

"abaich puinnsean
Ghin do ghràin
A-nis tha mi a 'tilgeil an duine seo gu dùsgadh"

She hissed, falling to her grey humanoid knees and casting her taloned hands wide. The poisonous magical plume rose above her spiking into a spray of fireworks that rained down in globs of goo before her massive wings whipped them against the green tinted wall of fire surrounding them.

"Akantha You alright? Have you gone too far, hurt yourself?" Questioned the flabby skinned fairy with a chin horn more befitting a goat.

Jhonathan watched warily as the two fairy's came to stand over him, his body still too weak to move, but his system no longer poisoned or bespelled, and his stomach full. He stared up at the two faces, one more beautiful than any fairy he had ever seen and the other oddly enthralling, with her fae realm deadliness harbouring large empathic eyes.

"Rest human. In time you will heal." The fairy called Akantha commanded, slinking to the dirt a mere foot away from him, her leathery wings stabbing into the earth creating a barrier between them.

Looking at the remaining fairy warily as she stood over him smiling with a fanged overbite

Jhonathan tried to smile back unsuccessfully, instead a mumble of words drifted from his parched lips.

"Water."

The fairy tilted her head, her rusty afro curls bouncing as she blinked her overly large eyes, the sideways eyelids shuttering momentarily, sending shivers down his spine. Pulling a skin flask from the belt around her waist she crouched close to him, her roasted nuts and garlic scent a lingering appeal as she pressed the throat of the flask to his lips.

Jhonathan drank deeply, unafraid of the odd-looking fairy for reasons he could not fathom except a deep instinct willing him to trust her. Maybe she held the power to enthral? Good for her. He thought, frowning as words fell from his open mouth, "She needed to she was so ugly." Wide-eyed and gasping beneath the onslaught of the water flask emptied onto his head he watched the fairy stand, turning her back on him, her shoulders shaking as she rounded her friends wing and disappeared behind it with a snuffle.

Movement of his limbs slowly returned to him as the night drew on. The light from the wall of fire never dimming as his thoughts raced around the words that left a subtle green tear in the corner of the fairy's eye before she turned from him. *Why the hell had he said that? He sure hadn't mean to.* The fairy would never help his plans to fruition if he couldn't control his tongue.

Sometime during the night, he had fallen under sleeps heavy influence, his water-soaked body growing cold with the passing time. Deep in dream, his mind was once again in the Seelie court, a bit in his mouth and a leash circling his throat. He knelt shirtless on the floor at the Queen's feet, gazing out at the amphitheatre of sorts where nobles who disobeyed her royal highness, were locked in vicious combat with the rulers most prized pet. The noble fairy's sword slashed a ribbon of blood down one scaly arm of the beast. It roared. Leapt forward in a splay of limbs and swift wing strokes – then bit his head clean off.

Jhonathan remembered his heart jack, as the humoured Queen smiled and mocked the headless noble. He hadn't meant to but the shock of it all had a gasp strangle from around his bit. That's when the Queens' eyes blinked at him with her sideways eyelids. She had smiled; and he truly knew fear for the next three days, he had endured tortures of all kinds, until the slightest murmur was banished from him under their horrific ministrations. Now the only moaning he did was in his sleep, like now, his leg was itching. Heating. Burning!

His eyes flew open to see his leg stretched through the wall of fire just as two menacing red ones locked on his from the shadows and a sharp pain like multiple daggers clamped his foot.

5. Fairy's

Shayleigh woke up at the strange mumblings of the human only to see him clawing at the earth as his body slid through her protective fire. *Why wasn't the creature screaming? Did it not require help?* She scuttled closer, staying low to the ground so she didn't upset him with her; ugliness.

She looked like the back of a sting ray gliding across sand, apart from the orange flame of her curls. She cocked her head, her silver eyes meeting the human's, lurching back as an arm suddenly extended to her, its hand grasping in her direction desperately. His body became visible at the torso as he was dragged backwards through the fire wall.

"H-elp!"

No sooner had he said the words the bat fairy had risen into the sky, eyes ablaze as her silver hair whipped behind her like forming storm clouds. "Shayleigh hold you're fire spell; I will deal with the

Kelpie!" And without a pause she flew into the wall just as the flames retracted into themselves, the other fairy spinkicked a circle into the dirt, chanting at the speed of magic as the wall of flame fell revealing a shadow horse blacker than ink. Its white tomb teeth sunken into the frayed flesh of the human's foot, his hot blood bubbling from around its lips, hot steaming water scolding from its nostrils as it snorted, shaking its river dredged mane.

Akantha took aim with the deadly tips of her sharp leather wings and arced down to slash at the Kelpie head, missing by inches as it shook its prey, tossing it aside. Its front hoofs stopped her wing strikes as it reared a fishy tale barbed with enormous poison tipped spines. She flew into the air again, veering down on the beast as it turned left to retrieve its prey, clawing in the open-air, shrieking in pain and smashing at Akantha with its barbed fishy tail.

"Uh, uh, uh." Shayleigh smiled revealing her large fangs before clawing into its opposite side, slashing her talons until the creature's tail fell as dead as its heart.

Blood speckled and sweaty the fairy's stood together, staring down at the silently brave human.

"It utters not a sound." Shayleigh remarked, licking a speck of blood from her fang as she knelt down next to the human, unsure as to whether it would flee or not. She held out a palm like she was coaxing a wildling, smiling her encouragement instead of sniffing her, as she expected, it put its hand in hers. She grinned, careful not to touch him with her accursed chin horn. But the human did not rise, its foot a lead weight of mangled flesh beneath the ministrations of the Kelpies teeth. Shayleigh pierced her lips as Akantha groomed gore from her wing spikes, baring the briefest of glances in their direction.

"We must take it back." Akantha insisted, coming to stand over her friend as Shayleigh administered a healing orb of magic and force-fed it to the human, who twisted and withered in pain until his body could take no more, passing out. Shayleigh frowned.

"That's not happened before." She mused, staring at the humans glowing open mouth.

"You've not healed a pet of the Queens before." Akantha stated bluntly. "I hear what they did to you was something these pets refer to as compassion; under our Queens' rule."

Shayleigh rose fluidly, eyes ablaze. "What do you know of what they did to me?" she roared, baring her fangs.

"Shay, I never meant to hurt you. I just thought maybe the human had more injuries than are visible to us and that's what's taking the magic so long to heal." Akantha looked down to the left, apologising again.

Calming her fury Shayleigh patted the shoulder of her friend, forgiving in a fleeting moment before turning back to the human she was so curious about. "Do you think you could carry him?"

"Carry the human? At night?" She raised an eyebrow looking at her friend's calm demeanour once again.

"Oh, come on, what are you afraid of?"

"Fine. I suppose I am already awake," she snapped, lifting the human like a rag doll in her arms and stretching her bendable wings to take flight. They navigated the trunks of trees as she watched Shayleigh scuttle up a large woody pine and leap out into the air, her arm skins flaring to catch the magic she used to help her glide when there was barely a breeze.

6. Jhonathan

When, he woke, the agony from his foot had dissipated. He flexed it slightly, confused as he roused feeling better than he had since the day he had been lured to the Fae realm and away from his life, his friends, and his family.

He stretched his spine, the vertebra popping deliciously instead of grinding like unoiled gears jammed together from the torture he had suffered. His bruised and damaged body had been thoroughly cleansed of injury, even his aching lungs no longer bothered him. And to think that a fairy had healed him!

The thought slipped his mind as he rolled to his side where the same fairy was kicking at a stone rimmed fire. The wildwoods were no longer in sight as the sun slowly rose over the hill where distantly he could make out the ominous imposition of the Seelie Queen's palace.

He shook his head, his voice coming to him in gasps, his pitch-black hair whipping at his face. "No!" He raged, scrambling to his feet and backing away, palms out to the fairy extinguishing the fire. "I can't go back there." He shook his head fiercely, a single digit stabbing at the distant Spector. The fairy cocked her head to one side, stumbling in his haste. "I won't!" He bellowed, turning to run but suddenly a taloned fist struck his face, knocking him to his back, four red streaks slashed across his cheek, their sting making his eyes water as the fire fairy stood in front of him. Her stance tense as she confronted her friend *-for him? Or in order to reap the reward the Queen would so graciously pay for the return of her enslaved pet?*

The two fairy's stood arguing but Jhonathan was too desperate to escape to listen to their quarrel. He knew they could stop him, but he had to try. Crawling to his feet, and dusting himself off in mock acceptance he sprinted for a neighbouring field to the left. It was full of what appeared to be hay bales; *somewhere he could disappear*, he thought, and not be too close to either the palace or the fairy's. He ran faster than he had ever run before, his arms and legs pumping with adrenalin as he ran down hill, his feet skidding beneath him as his body struggled to keep its balance.

The field of hay bales wasn't much further and even with the wind stinging the marks lashed across his face he had never felt stronger. The fairy's healing magic rejuvenated his body, mind and soul. Skidding before hitting the next hill at full velocity Jhonathan daren't look behind him. The damn fairy's could fly over the valley he had to run through. They could already be at the top waiting to trap him. But somehow, he made it. Straight to the top without diversion or interception. His feet pummelled the harsh fae grass. A wooden fence surrounded the baled harvest of the field he desperately ran towards. Without thinking and at full pelt he vaulted the fence, instantly disappearing behind a hay bale, weaving his way from mound to mound out of the sight of the fairy's.

7. Fairy's

Shayleigh glared at Akantha, hands on her hips, her cheeks puffed out like a hoarding squirrel. "Alright, fine." She conceded. "Keep him!" She threw her wings up in the air. "But the Queen's wrath will rain down on us if she even suspects our involvement." With that she pushed off into the sky, leaving Shayleigh to walk to the field the human had escaped to.

Maybe that will give her some time to think about what she's doing, Akantha flapped her leathery wings. She was glad there were no trees Shayleigh could launch herself from with the aid of her magic to fly. Akantha needed her space, especially right now, when her rage was getting the better of her, her fangs and talons were lengthening, and a deep lust for vengeance for pitting her only friend against her, was seething from her every pore.

The field wasn't far and the human's stamina couldn't compare to a fairy's so she had no doubt she would recapture him. The selfish creature; running from them when they saved his miserable human life. She had carried him. Cradled him for seelie sake! The filthy thing. It would take weeks to scrub its stench from her skin.

A fairy's eye view gave her the leverage of surprise when she dropped soundlessly from the sky to land behind a perfectly formed bale of seya hay. Suddenly a flawless plan of vengeance that would not physically damage the human she swore not to destroy. But she never promised Shayleigh that she would stop him. She smiled wickedly, tracking the creature's stench and appearing before him, fangs long enough to cleave a head, claws raking at the seya bale, sparks of grain spraying from their granite touch.

Frantically the human skidded to a halt, turned and ran to her right, several small bales hiding him from sight. Akantha's grin widened as silently she ran, her wings speeding her way the slightest of hums.

Out popped the human, straight before her, an expression of horror on his slashed and weeping face.

He hit the dirt. His decent was beyond his control as he frantically scrambled, turning as he came to his feet. Akantha laughed, the sound of knife blades tinkling to the floor a rough contrast with her granite talons sliding up the side of the bales. Grain sparked behind her like the remnants of a chain saw as she pursued him, all the while leading the stupid human to the destination of her choosing. A place that if all went well would ensure the safety of both herself and Shayleigh.

8. Jhonathan

Jhonathan was being herded, he knew it, but he couldn't stop the flight that sent his legs pumping in a bid to escape the psychotic fairy with talons that were twice the size he had seen them last, and fangs like sabre tooth tigers. It didn't help that she smiled as he ran, that she pursued him with that grating voice fairy's used to ensnare their victims. He had no choice. He had to run. Or they would return him to the Queen; he would rather die.

His face ached, the wounds trickling down his pale skin as adrenaline pumped his blood pressure to new heights. He was being hunted, stalked, like a cat would torment a mouse – this was what the fairy's called games, this was how they had fun -oh God!

He had stumbled from behind another bale and fallen down into the pits of hell. He eyes blanked, his mind screaming to nonchalance as he accepted the fact that, anyone in the Queen's amphitheatre, would.

9. Fairy's

When Shayleigh finally caught up to Akantha she was staring off into the distance, a seemingly calm expression painting her dark face. She had expected her to be half dragging the human back with her, her anger severe enough to have her massive fangs showing, her talons raking the dirt she trod with their uncomfortable weight. But Akantha was fine. Calm, too calm. And where in the name of Seelie was the human? Her human? "What. Have. You. Done?"

Akantha regarded her stoically. "Nothing that you shouldn't have done. Besides, I kept my word." She waved a hand nonchalantly. "I didn't harm it."

Shayleigh stormed off through the bales, the tinkling of Akantha's voice carrying to her on the slight breeze- "You're welcome!"

Welcome, she snorted. *Who in the name of Seelie did Akantha think she was, getting rid of her new-found human?* She was becoming quite attached to the pet. *No*, she thought, *the Queens pet. No. My. Pet.*

She stomped through the splintered grain, no doubt from *someone's* cutting administrations. Thundered around three more humped bales before sniffing the human's stench on the air. He was close, very close if the strength of his scent told her anything, but the notes of it had altered, fragrances of citrus and sour berry now layered it.

Shayleigh was careful as she walked further and further until a long row of bales fell away at the edge of the field and beyond it hissed the snores of a fairy battle dragon lost to madness in its age. It was Queen kept as her most favoured hunting toy. She loved sports, but hunting was her speciality, and she very much enjoyed watching the dragon of her four fathers entertain her with its vicious dissection of its convicted prey. However, the Queen's pet was only guilty of escaping and trying to return home. He had recently become Shayleigh's pet, in her opinion, and *she really needed to put a leash on him*, she thought. *The silly thing was getting himself into all kinds of danger running around like a drunken pixie.* She sighed, her sharp eyes roaming over the charred, rock spiked valley the dragon dwell in. She would have to be careful if she went down there, for even though she might best the dragon, the Queen and her guards at the palace could appear on her balcony over the valley at any second and then- she would be as good as dead; like the rest of her family.

She couldn't believe Akantha would do this, although the fairy was just trying to protect her, she didn't understand the pull of power calling to her when she was with the human. The intrigue was too strong to deny. She had to get him back, she just had to.

Jumping down to the scorched valley below, her skin flaps catching air currents, she glided above looking out for the human with dark hair amongst the grey mottled stalactites, remembering not to get too close to the cave at the valley's centre. The cave where puffs of smoke bellowed like a forest fire from inside.

That's when she spied him out in the open instead of hiding. *See Akantha,* she thought. *He wanted to be found, to be saved.* She watched him crouch next to a coal dark rock, his head bowed. Landing gently beside him she crouched, cocking her head at the blackened mass.

10. Jhonathan

Jhonathan touched the blackened ashes appearing like rock in their surroundings, but he knew better. It was the P.E.T empathisers. He knew because he had pulled the odd shaped pin they always wore from the ashes, twisting it over and under his fingers as he prayed for their souls. The light step of the fairy next to him didn't startle him. He had already accepted his fate as he chose it and that would be death by roasting in the inferno of the dragon's fire. Not via the Queen's hand. The fairy knelt next to him, her head cocked to one side, her forefinger gently stroking her curled chin horn. She gazed from the blackened mass barely a bone survived to him, her brow furrowing. But still, she did not speak. Merely held her taloned hand out to him and waited.

Jhonathan didn't know what he should do. The fairy's that helped him escape the Queen were here, scorched to death by the dragon, no doubt her guards had been too busy rounding them up for execution to go after him. And now a blasted fairy held her hand out to him, for what? So, she could fly them to the amphitheatre? From what he understood this fairy had to climb something high before she could glide on the wind or use her magic for currents and the only thing that large inside the dragon's valley, was its cave.

11. Fairy's

The human crouched, glaring at Shayleigh. He didn't take her hand, merely stared, transfixed on the charred remains. The small badge rolling between his fingers, stuck in some kind of remorseful thrall. But there was no time to spare as the earth beneath their feet started to quake with the onslaught of heavy thuds emanating from the caves entrance. They were close enough that if the dragon's head popped out then they would surely be targeted for a flambé dinner.

Shayleigh spun to her feet, grabbing the human's arm in time to twist him behind her as she ran, half dragging her new pet. But a few scrapes and bruises were better than being burnt to death; weren't they? The human uttered not a sound but his body clumsily tripping along behind her rang out like an orchestra in the Queen's court.

She cringed as the vibrations of the earth beneath their feet took on a new beat. A thrum increasing in speed, the ground shook harder as it hunted them, its long mossy green tail whipping around a rock to their left. Shayleigh turn abruptly, her eyes glowing, aventurine, chanting;

"teine na beatha
gairmidh mi ort
tilg dhomh do bholtaichean
leig seachad do sholas an-asgaidh."

And the fire formed from her open palm. The human gaped, his eyes returning to life until before them the dragon, its scales dulled by the crusting coat of blood splatters, hunkered down ready to pounce. But Shayleigh would not be one of them and neither would her human; she hoped. She knelt to one knee, releasing her hold on his, to balance her aim as she shot bolt after bolt at the dragons' eyes, until he opened his gaping maw to return her strikes in a tornado of blazing fire.

12. Jhonathan

Smoke obscured his view of the landscape. But even so Jhonathan knew that the dragons cave was North-East of them, for the Queen's palace spires could be seen above the smog of the battling fairy's. This was his one and only chance. He felt guilty about leaving the fairy to fight the dragon alone, but really, what could he do? Besides, she might protect him now, but the only one who could free them from the sheer depth of the valley was the Queen herself, and he was sure she would enjoy the sport of the dragon hunting them, then releasing them.

So, he took off, to the very pace the Queen's pet legendized as they spoke of hope in hushed whispers in the dead of night. A place he never thought he would see again; home. But first he had to get through the smoke choking his lungs and stinging his eyes. He fell to his already weathered knees, thanks to being dragged like a rag doll behind the fairy, and silently thanked his mother for the fire drills she would insist they learnt, as being in a house fire herself she had made sure her brood would be prepared in case of any such mishaps happening again. Okay, so she was a little obsessed, he smiled to himself, he couldn't wait to see her.

Crawling hand and feet over the rocks, skittering as fast as he could in the smoke fogged valley, he spotted the cave, well at least he hoped it was the cave- for all he could see it might end out to be a deep crevasse. But luck was with him and as he crawled on bloodied hands and knees into the caves entrance, he could see the shinning portal of hope materialise as in legend, before him.

Only a few strides through a mountain of half charred carcases separated him.

13. Fairy's

Shayleigh was furious. During the time it took her to cast fire bolts to engage the dragon, her aim to disappear into the rocky maze as soon as he shot back, hidden around the smoke of his foul breath, her pet had vanished. The damn human was a coward, and she really should leave his ass to get fired but just thinking about it made her heart clench, small as it was. The poor thing couldn't help it if he was senseless as well as stupid.

Dodging left as the dragon reared towards her, close enough for her to measure her height against his teeth, Shayleigh ran after her human, noticing that to her utter distress the thing proved to be stupider than she had thought possible when he turned to enter the dragon's cave.

"Oh, for Seelie's sake!" she screamed like a banshee, her talons clicking a constant rhythm as the ground beneath her shook with the dragon's loping pursuit, a steady stream of fire oscillated from its open jaw, just inches from lighting behind.

At the cave mouth, she too skidded to a halt then nipped inside before the dragon could make her a tappas. She rounded the entrance, expecting it to slow, its size so vast, it looked to be a tight fit, but she was sadly mistaken. The dragon stopped breathing tunnels of fire, instead adopting a predatorial smile as it recognised its prey was trapped.

Shayleigh ran up to her human, sending up black puffs of charred remains in her wake as she feebly tried to navigate them without injury. He was on his knees when she got to him, prodding the lower right section of a portal she had no idea existed in here. Her human might be stupid, but he was defiantly good at finding escape routes. Shayleigh knocked him aside with a huff, but he would not release his feverish grip on the portal. Cursing she stared behind her, the dragons' teeth scrapped at her waist, his hot breath bubbling the human's skin as he desperately clawed at the portal.

"Human." She gritted, her fangs lengthening as the dragon licked his tongue out to taste her. "Let. Go. Of. The. Portal. No!" she roared, her eyes glowing a shocking green that sparked flares, momentarily blinding the beast before slapping an open palm onto the portal, her magic flowing through her.

The dragon bellowed its rage. A wind whipped up in the cave. The portal glowed. Shayleigh grabbed her pet. Then the dragon opened its jaws and-

SNAP!

14. Jhonathan

He couldn't believe it. They had tumbled through the portal at such velocity thanks to Akantha who slammed into them full force from above the dragon's head, that blood skids of green, blue and red hissed on the wet tarmac of an alley abandoned to waste. His back screamed in agony. But he couldn't deny the gratitude he had for the fairy Akantha. Without her he would have been inside the mouth of the dragon, ground to dust among its teeth. As it was, the beasts foremost tooth stood like a shard from the portal Shayleigh was busy closing.

Two large green eyes glared at him, and yet he could do nothing but smile, earning the strange incomprehension of the fairy's tilt of her head as the portal snapped shut, disguising itself like a chameleon against the alley wall. She waved a hand over the tooth protruding from the entrance and it too vanished.

Jhonathan knew he had lost too much blood to survive. Knew he had earned the green-eyed fairy's rage for leaving her alone at the mercy of the dragon. But what he did not expect, were her eyes to shift, morphing into that of a human as her fairy self cast a glamour – appearing as an awkward looking teenager with chubby round cheeks, a full stomach and stumpy arms. Her chin was two sizes too big and gnarled at the end like at some point she had had immensely bad acne.

His mouth dropped open, his head turning to the side. Akantha sat next to the alley wall, a trail of blue blood speckling the path where she had dragged her self. Jhonathan watched as Shayleigh walked towards her, the heavy rainfall pounding like spears into his chest. She grew an orb of green magic, casting it into her friends open mouth. Abruptly she turned to glare down at him. Another shinning orb in her palm. She batted it up and down as she thought, all the while staring expectantly into his eyes. His eyes that were heavy with pain, his lids full of oppressing fatigue.

Then he felt the sour taste of her magic upon his tongue, the all-consuming adrenaline burst healing every scratch and tear. Masterfully stitching every bone and damaged vertebra a thousand times faster than the very first time she saved him from the poisonous fruit of the Puinnsean tree.

Blinking twice Jhonathan opened his eyes to two human looking fairy's staring down at him and smiled as he reached into his pocket, pulling from it a small badge. Holding it out to the slender, grey haired girl next to him. Shayleigh's eyes shone from behind her human glamour as her best friend accepted her pets' gift; and so, the P.E.T empathisers were reborn.

Call to action

If you enjoyed this book then follow me on; https://linktr.ee/carrie_weston

And if you enjoyed this book then please leave a review on; https://www.goodreads.com/author/show/19206998.Carrie_Weston

Pronunciation

Jhonathan (silent h)

Akantha (ah-can-tha)

Shayleigh (Sh-ahy-lee)

Seya (say-ah)

Printed in Great Britain
by Amazon